Other Books in the Series

ZARA'S BIG MESSY DAY
ZARA'S BIG MESSY BEDTIME
ZARA'S BIG MESSY GOODBYE

Complete your "Big Messy" collection at
www.WheatPennyPress.com

ZARA'S BIG MESSY
Playdate

BY REBEKAH BORUCKI
ART BY DANIELLE PIOLI

Rebekah "Bex" Borucki, founder of BEXLIFE® and the BLISSED IN® wellness movement, is a mother of five, meditation guide, and author of books for big and little readers. Rebekah also founded WPP Little Readers Big Change Initiative, Inc., a publicly-funded 501(c)(3) registered nonprofit, which provides free books, mental wellness tools, and writing workshops for students in grades PreK-8, public libraries, and community organizations. Rebekah loves volunteering at her kids' book fairs where she always buys lots of books for herself. **www.BexLife.com/zara**

Danielle Pioli is a multi-passionate artist and certified hypnotherapist who helps artists and creatives navigate their creativity so they can heal what's been holding them back and thrive—even through chaos. **www.DaniellePioli.com**

Illustrated by Danielle Pioli
Edited by Esther Goldenberg and Winona Platt
Author photo by Justin Borucki; Illustrator photo courtesy of Danielle Pioli
Original design for Worry the Dragon by Megan Conway Lapp (www.craftyintentions.net)

First edition April 2021 — Published by Wheat Penny Press — Printed in China
ISBN: 978-1-7362410-1-1; electronic book ISBN: 978-1-7362410-5-9

Fonts used in the design of this book: Oscar Bravo, New Beginnings, and Sofia Pro Soft
The artwork was created digitally, using Adobe Photoshop and pen display by Wacom MobileStudio Pro

THIS BOOK WAS WRITTEN DURING A BIG MESSY YEAR THAT MADE US
FIND NEW WAYS OF LEARNING, WORKING, AND STAYING CONNECTED WHEN
WE HAD TO BE SO VERY FAR APART. IT'S DEDICATED TO THE INCREDIBLE
STUDENTS AND TEACHERS WHO MADE MAGIC OUT OF THE MESSY AND
INSPIRED ME TO KEEP CREATING GOOD THINGS FOR THEM.

It was Friday afternoon, but Zara and her little brother, Sam, were thinking about Saturday.

Tomorrow was the big book fair.

Zara was excited to help sell books.

Sam was excited to buy new comics.

"Kids, it's time to clean up!

I have a surprise for you!"

A surprise?

What is Mama talking about?

Sam wasn't as curious as Zara.

"Oh good, they're here! Mrs. Relish is helping me plan for the fair, and she brought Penelope along for a playdate!"

Mrs. Relish? Penelope? Oh no, not Penelope Relish! Zara was mortified.

Penelope Relish was Zara's playground nemesis. A playdate with Penelope was Mama's worst idea ever!

"Have fun, kids!"

Zara was stuck.

Penelope made herself at home.

She banged on Sam's drums and swiped
all the best crayon colors.

And when they played grocery store,
Penelope made herself the boss.

Zara was done with this playdate.

Before long, it was time for Mrs. Relish and Penelope to go.

"See you tomorrow!" Penelope shouted.

"Tomorrow?" Zara asked.

"At the book fair," Mama replied.

"Won't that be fun?"

It will *not!* Zara scowled
at the thought.

It was Saturday morning—book fair day!

Zara had forgotten all about her Penelope problem and got busy making posters.

Penelope showed up with the same idea.

"Oh, you started without me," Penelope remarked.

"That's okay. I can fix these posters for you."

Fix? What is there to fix? Zara was annoyed, but she kept quiet.

"*I* will draw the pictures because *I'm* a better artist. *You* can color. Make sure you stay in the lines!"

Zara let out a huff but went along
with Penelope's plan.

It was time to open shop!

Mrs. Relish gave Zara and Penelope a very important job: working at the checkout table.

Zara and Penelope's second-grade class just learned how to count money, so they went to work.

Zara had enough.

"You are not the boss of me, Penelope Relish!
And we're not friends, either!"

Dr. Rampersad, one of Zara and Penelope's class moms, heard Zara shouting.

"Girls, what is happening over here?" she asked.

"Penelope said I was stupid and that I color like a baby! She took all the jobs and wouldn't let me do anything!" Zara blurted out.

"I did not! I'm just better at drawing and counting. I was helping!"

"I see," said Dr. Rampersad. "Can we talk?"

The girls agreed.

"It seems like you're both upset. I have a tool that I use with people who come to me for help when they're upset. I think it might work for you, too. Let's take a couple of big breaths first."

"I'm going to tell you about **wants, worries, boundaries,** and **big dreams**. You can use these words to help you talk instead of argue."

First, talk about your WANTS. It sounds like Zara wants to help with the book fair. And it sounds like Penelope wants the same.

Then, share your WORRIES. Zara feels left out. She's worried she won't get to help with the book fair. Penelope is worried that you won't do a good job.

Build a BOUNDARY. Boundaries are rules we make up for how we want people to treat us, so we don't get hurt—like a fence that protects a garden from getting trampled. Zara's boundary might be that she doesn't want you to tell her what to do. Penelope might like a rule about picking jobs before you start.

"Did I get that right, Zara?" Dr. Rampersad asked. Zara nodded.

"And how do you feel about what I said, Penelope?"

"All right, I guess," Penelope shrugged.

And now, share your BIG DREAMS! What if you could turn your problem into a wish come true? Maybe that looks like doing a job, each in your own way, and making this book fair the best one ever!

The girls agreed and got back to work, but it wasn't long before Penelope forgot all about Dr. Rampersad's lesson.

Zara felt like she might explode!

But instead of shouting, she took a deep breath and used Dr. Rampersad's words.

TOTAL $$$

talk about my wants

"Penelope, I want to count change, too," Zara began.

share my worries

"I don't like that you keep taking over."

build a boundary

"If you want to work together, you have to stop telling me what to do."

share my big dreams

"Let's have fun and raise a lot of money for our school!"

Penelope let out a huff and mumbled "fine" under her breath.

Good enough, thought Zara.

Zara and Penelope spent the rest of the afternoon mostly getting along.

Zara had to remind Penelope about boundaries once or twice, but that didn't bother Zara. She felt good about speaking up for herself.

A NOTE FOR PARENTS, CAREGIVERS, AND EDUCATORS

from the author, Rebekah Borucki

I love the scenario in this book because it's so relatable. There have been times when I've played the part of Zara, but many others when I've shown up like Penelope. And as a parent, there have been countless times when I've had to be Dr. Rampersad for my kids.

Years ago, my friend introduced me to a conversation method that she and her husband were using in their business. I was intrigued and put it to use immediately. I was so impressed by its impactful but straightforward steps that I started sharing it with everyone I knew. In *Zara's Big Messy Playdate*, Dr. Rampersad uses an adapted version of the method to teach Zara and Penelope (and your child) how to achieve peaceful, compassionate conflict resolution.

How to Use the Method in *Zara's Big Messy Playdate*

from Alexandra Jamieson and Bob Gower, co-authors of *Radical Alignment*

We're delighted for this opportunity to share our **All-In Method (AIM)** with you. Here's how you can help your little one(s) practice the method easily and effectively.

Set the scene by inviting your child(ren) to talk through the four steps: **Wants**, **Worries**, **Boundaries**, and **Big Dreams** (what we call Intentions, Concerns, Boundaries, and Dreams in our book for adults, *Radical Alignment*—get a free chapter at RadicalAlignmentBook.com). Choose a time when you're both fed and rested. As adults, we avoid important conversations if we are tired, hungry, emotionally overwhelmed, or otherwise distracted.

Agree to the topic to be discussed, and make time for each person to share their **Wants**, **Worries**, **Boundaries**, and **Big Dreams**. Parties must agree to take turns, listen, and not talk over each other.

It's okay to ask open-ended questions that help your child to express themselves. Two questions that help us find our **Boundaries** are: "What do you need to feel safe in this situation?" and "What do you need to feel your best about this?" Let everyone know that they may not get everything they want and that it's vital that everyone feels included.

Get Creative and Make the All-In Method Work for You

We've used the four-step **All-In Method** conversation as a family on topics ranging from vacation plans to the new school year, screen time rules to a family crisis. Please feel encouraged to use this book in a way that serves your family's specific needs.

Write it out. Spending quiet time to write out our thoughts is a helpful way for people, big or little, to get clear on their feelings. You can use each step of the method as a writing (or drawing) prompt. Encourage your child to share, but be sure to listen without judgment—for your child and yourself. Let them know that it's also okay to keep their feelings to themselves, as long as you feel safe with that option.

Use the All-In Method as a way to connect daily. You don't have to do all parts of the method each time but can use one element—like **Wants**—to start a conversation. Then follow the thread with your child. "You're going to a museum with your class tomorrow? What do you want to see or experience there?"

Hold up a mirror. You can also use the method by mirroring your child's feelings back to them. You could say something like, "It sounds like you're worried about _____." Then let them give you feedback on your assessment.

Let us know how it's working! Contact us at support@radicalalignmentbook.com or visit RadicalAlignmentBook.com for cheat sheets, a free chapter, and more. Stay in touch with Zara on Instagram @ZarasBigMessyBooks or at BigMessyBooks.com. Bonus learning materials and resources are available at BexLife.com/zara-bonus.